All This Intimacy

by Rajiv Joseph

A SAMUEL FRENCH ACTING EDITION

SAMUEL FRENCH

FOUNDED 1830

New York Hollywood London Toronto

SAMUELFRENCH.COM

ISBN 978-0-573-63394-2   Printed in U.S.A.   #185

BILLING AND CREDIT REQUIREMENTS

All producers of ALL THIS INTIMACY *must* give credit to the Author of the Play and the Author of the Novel in all programs distributed in connection with performances of the Play and in all instances in which the title of the Play appears for purposes of advertising, publicizing or otherwise exploiting the Play and/or a production. The name of the Author of the Play *must* appear on a separate line on which no other name appears, immediately following the title, and *must* appear in size of type not less than fifty percent the size of the title type. The name of the Author of the Novel must appear on a separate line immediately below the Name of the Author of the Play in a size of type equal to that of the Author of the Play, wherever and whenever the Author of the Play receives credit.

All This Intimacy premiered in 2006 at the 2econdStage Theatre UPTOWN, Carole Rothman, Artistic Director and Ellen Richard, Interim Executive Director. The production was directed by Giovanna Sardelli with the following cast and production staff:

JEN...................................Gretchen Egolf
SETH...................................Adam Green
MAUREEN........................Amy Landecker
FRANNY.............................Kate Nowlin
BECCA...............................Krysten Ritter
TY.................................Thomas Sadoski

Sets by David Newell
Costumes by Amy Clark
Lighting by Rie Ono
Sound Design by Bart Fasbender
Production Stage Manager: Rachel J. Perlman
Stage Manager: Stephanie Atlan

CHARACTERS

TY, 30
JEN, 28
MAUREEN, 42
BECCA, 18
FRANNY, 26
SETH, 30

TIME

Present

PLACE

Brooklyn and Manhattan

For Katherine Berg

ACT I

Scene 1
No Joke

(TY and SETH in Ty's apartment.)

SETH. Please tell me this is a joke.

TY. It's not.

SETH. You're shitting me. I know you. You're shitting me.

TY. Seth, I'm telling you.

SETH. Okay! Okay, *Jen*. And the neighbor? That neighbor you were...? You were...?

TY. Yes. Maureen.

SETH. How *old* is she?

TY. She's forty-two.

SETH. Forty-two? She's *forty-two* years old?

TY. Yes, okay?

SETH. No, Ty, this is not happening. One girl. One girl. Jen.

TY. *Three*, Seth. *Three.*

SETH. No.

TY. Yes.

SETH. Jesus.

TY. I know.

SETH. Fuck!

TY. That's what I'm saying!

SETH. I don't understand. How can this happen?

TY. I don't know. I don't know!

SETH. This is messed up!

TY. What am I going to do?

SETH. And who else? You said three! Who's the third? Who's the third girl?

TY. You don't know her.

SETH. Well who is she?

TY. Why does it matter? I am in serious shit.

SETH. Some random girl? Who? Ty, who is it?

TY. I need you to not freak out on me.

SETH. Who's the third girl? Who's the third girl?!

(Beat)

TY. This girl... She's ... this ....

Scene 2
Hot Little Thing

(Lights up across the stage on BECCA who holds a notebook and faces the audience.)

BECCA.
I am standing on the precipice of my life
And life is such a confusion.

Why do I stand upon the edge with such wind around me?
What if I fall?
    (Beat; she lowers the paper and looks out.) Thank you.

Scene 3
Cum Laude

(Back to SETH and TY.)

    SETH. Your *student!?*
    TY. Seth...
    SETH. Your *student!?* Ty, your *student?!*
    TY. Just calm down.
    SETH. How old?
    TY. Seth...
    SETH. How old?
    TY. Eighteen.

(SETH freaks.)

    TY. Stop it.
    SETH. *Eighteen! Forty-two! Thirty!*
    TY. Jen's twenty-eight.
    SETH. Whatever!
    TY. Listen, Seth...
    SETH. Wait! Can you please just... tell me! You had sex

with three different women in one week!?

TY. It wasn't all the same week, it was like over a nine-day period.

SETH. That's dirty. That's extremely dirty.

TY. It just... happened.

SETH. What were you thinking?! Can you tell me that? What were you thinking??

Scene 4
Labyrinth

TY. *(To audience)* Two years ago I published a small book of poetry. It won a lot of awards. For a book of poetry, it did pretty good. It was called *Labyrinth*. People like it, I think, because even though it's a collection of poems, it tells one long narrative story, and the story is about a young man who finds out that he has super powers. But his superpowers are weird. Basically, he can make any place he goes into a labyrinth. If he is in a single hallway, he can create a hundred hallways out of it. If he is in a small house, he can create miles of catacombs and tunnels all around it. It makes no sense, this superpower. It defies all sorts of logic, and even for a made-up superpower, it raises a lot of bothersome questions. Anyhow, it was a cool book of poems. The book made me a little money and got me this teaching position at Columbia University, teaching a poetry workshop to undergraduates. The success of the book, and this pretty cool job, made me very confident about pretty much everything in general. *(He steps out on to his back porch which is littered with shiny, colorful toys for a small child.)*

And then one day I stepped out on to my back porch in Brooklyn to find a bunch toys lying around for no reason at all.

Scene 5
Little Kid Toys

(TY crouches down, picking up a brightly colored ball. He stares at the ball and the other toys with wonder.
MAUREEN enters from the apartment next door. She sees TY with all the toys.)

MAUREEN. Excuse me. What the hell are you doing?

TY. I'm playing with toys.

MAUREEN. Those toys belong to my son.

TY. I didn't take them, they were here.

MAUREEN. Where'd you get them?!

TY. I'm sorry! I just came out on my porch and I found all these toys here. They were sitting here.

MAUREEN. Oh. I'm sorry... I ... I don't know why... My son must have done this. He's being difficult today. I'm sorry. I'm a little crazy.

TY. Here, you can have them back.

MAUREEN. No, I'm sorry I snapped at you.
TY. These are nice toys.
MAUREEN. Yeah, they're nice.
TY. I love this ball!

(MAUREEN looks at the ball. She puts her hands out and TY tosses it to her. She catches it.)

TY. I'm Ty.
MAUREEN. Maureen.
TY. You just moved in here?
MAUREEN. Back in August.
TY. It was really something coming out and finding all these toys here. It was ... I don't know, it was magical in a way.
MAUREEN. You like toys, huh?
TY. No, I mean, there was a quality about coming out here and finding a pile of beautiful toys just waiting for me. Like my childhood sitting out here reminding me of something.
I think I had this exact ball. *(Beat)* I'm sorry. I probably sound weird. I get like this a lot these days. These are beautiful, these toys. They're so new.
MAUREEN. We just bought them. We were all set to adopt. A girl. We'd gone through the whole process seven years ago with Augustus, my son. But this time we backed out at the last minute.
TY. I'm sorry. Why'd you back out?
MAUREEN. Well, we kind of came to the conclusion... that... My husband... My husband.

(MAUREEN tosses the ball to him. They play catch.)

TY. It's funny these back porches.

MAUREEN. Why?

TY. We're so close together. It's like we share it. But we never interact. Nobody does, I mean. Nobody ever talks or anything, even though we're all so close.

MAUREEN. It's city life.

TY. I've never met you or your kid. Or your husband...?

MAUREEN. Nick.

TY. I haven't met him either.

MAUREEN. He doesn't really like the back porch. He thinks they're all too close together.

TY. It's city life.

MAUREEN. I don't mind it.

TY. I don't mind it either. It's intimate.

MAUREEN. That's one way of looking at it.

TY. In that distant way.

MAUREEN. The closer you get with someone, the further apart you get. I mean... I don't know what I mean. I'm sorry. I feel a little crazy.

TY. You don't seem that crazy.

MAUREEN. Well, you should get to know me.

TY. I should.

MAUREEN. Soon you'd be running for the hills.

TY. Well, anytime you want to get away from your craziness, hop on over.

MAUREEN. Just hop on over.

TY. Yeah. You know, whatever.

MAUREEN. Just hop on over.

TY. We can defeat the paradox of city life.

MAUREEN. Oh yeah? We can be intimate without being

distant?

TY. We can be anything you want.

MAUREEN. Really.

TY. Sure.

MAUREEN. That's very bold of you, *Ty*. I don't know quite how I feel about that.

TY. I'm just a friendly neighbor.

MAUREEN. You're certainly more than that. Are you always this friendly?

TY. No. But the spirit moves me.

MAUREEN. The spirit, huh? I have to go take care of my kid.

TY. You want your toys back?

MAUREEN. Maybe I'll come get them later.

(She smiles and exits. TY turns to the audience.)

TY. About a week later we were just talking, she was over there, she had been digging in the garden, and she was all sweaty and she came over to the railing and we started talking and I could see right through her shirt. Anyhow, I was smoking a cigarette, and she asked if she could have a drag. She doesn't smoke, she says, but she just wants a drag, but her hands are muddy from the garden, so I take the cigarette in my fingers and hold it to her lips. And ... then... God ... Damn...

(MAUREEN enters, grabs TY, they have sex.)

MAUREEN. Hey.

TY. Hey. How you doing?

MAUREEN. Fine
TY. Yeah?
MAUREEN. Yeah.
TY. Good.
MAUREEN. Yeah. You?
TY. Fine.
MAUREEN. Good.
TY. Good.

(They finish. MAUREEN exits. TY stumbles downstage, pulling up his pants, finally falling to the ground, spent.)

TY. *(To audience)* Anyhow. Really liked it. Really liked it. I mean. Yeah, it was good.

Scene 6
Laryngitis

(TY's apartment.)

JEN. Ty... I wasn't going to bring this up today, but seeing as you have laryngitis, I figured this might be the best time to have this conversation. Because any inclination you might have to interrupt me, well, that just won't be possible because you can't speak. Ha. Oh well. *(TY gets up, pulls out a notebook, pen, and scribbles on a page.)*

Okay, okay... Just sit still for a second and let me speak before you start to scribbling away like a madman, jeez! I knew you'd do this or something, just sit and let me say my peace! *(JEN reads what he wrote.)*

Look, I know it is, but I kind of have to seize the moment here. Whenever we talk you always talk me out, you put words in my mouth. *(TY writes again and shows the page. JEN reads.)*

No! That's NOT what I mean! *(TY hits himself in the face with the notebook.)*

Listen. *(TY gestures sarcastically.)*

Okay. Ty. *(Beat)*

So. As you know. As we both well know... There has never been a time in my life, really *ever*, when I haven't been, you know ... *in school*. And I know I'm always saying this, okay?

Let me finish! *(JEN reads the notebook. TY scrawls something brief. She reads.)*

You know I don't like that word, and it's rude. *(He scrawls another word, seemingly profane.)*

Nice. Thank you. Shut up.

Okay! God! I can't believe you have laryngitis and you're still interrupting me! Constantly! *(TY scrawls. JEN does not read.)*

Look, I'm going to talk and you can listen or you can not listen, but here it is. When it comes to figuring out what to do with my life, I've been seriously claustrophobic. Because choosing things narrows down your life, it limits you and it freaks me out. I'm not kidding. Every time you make a decision, you narrow your life more and more... I mean that's what you're supposed to do! It's about carving out an identity before you get old and die! *(TY scrawls.)*

No. NO! I don't want sushi! I'm not *staying* for *dinner!* *(TY scrawls.)*

BREAK UP, Okay? BREAK. UP. Me. Break Up. With You. How about that! Oh, but this has never happened to Ty Greene before because he's too smooth a talker and no one can ever get two words in—*(TY scrawls.)*

I'm not going to read your shit! *(TY writes. Shows her earnestly. She reads it in spite of herself. She looks at him and then away.)*

We've talked about this!

And don't look at me like that! *You* know. You have your book and your job and you're hot shit and all that, so you don't know what I'm talking about. *(TY scrawls "So?!" and shows her.)*

So that's it. And by the way, a year ago you broke up with me. Out of the blue! So don't act all heartbroken. *(TY looks at her, heartbroken.)*

Yeah yeah yeah. *(TY scrawls something, shows her.)*

Very funny.

No! I *don't* want that! That's what we've *been* doing. No more fooling around. No more hooking up. No more having your cake and eating it too. *(TY scrawls.)*

That's what I meant by cake.

It's not you. I just never feel that we're on the same page. *(TY rips a page from the notebook and throws it at JEN. He rips more out and throws them at JEN.)*

This is what I'm talking about, Ty. I'm trying to pull things together. I love you, but when I'm around you, things come apart.

They come apart.

(TY stares at JEN. He writes deliberately in his notebook for a long time. He throws the notebook at JEN, she picks it up, reads it, looks at TY, reads it again, takes out a pen, writes something, throws the book at him.
TY reads it, writes something, throws the notebook at her. Jen reads it, writes, throws the book, hits TY.
He reads, writes, hands her the book.
She reads it, laughs, smiles at him. She writes, throws the book at him.
He picks it up, reads, gets pissed, writes, throws it at her.
She reads, writes, walks over to him, gives the book to him. He reads. He writes something very brief, shows her, she reads, she slaps him.
They look at each other. He writes, she reads, she tosses the notebook aside. They make out.)

Scene 7
Seth Warns of Franny

(Back at Ty's apartment.)

SETH. How does a condom not work?

TY. How does it *ever* work is a better question. I mean they're made of LATEX. Shouldn't it rip? We rub it and roll it and pinch it and squeeze it and slap it around and it's still supposed to protect us!?

SETH. This is a huge mess.

TY. And it's supposed to be *thin*. Thin, so we can feel *through* it. So we can pretend it's not there.

SETH. I came over here, and I thought, *Jen is pregnant. This is a big mess.* But now you drop the other two on me, and I swear to God, Ty, you are so fucked. You are so so so fucked.

TY. I know.

SETH. I'm not going to lie to you.

TY. Thanks.

SETH. Look: Are you 100% certain with each one?

TY. What do you mean?

SETH. A: Do the other girls know for sure they're pregnant? And B: Are you absolutely certain you are the father?

TY. I'm pretty sure.

SETH. Well, "pretty sure" is not 100%.

TY. I'm pretty sure! I'm sure! I'm 100% sure.

SETH. Let me tell you something, man. Franny? Franny is out of her mind.

TY. I know...

SETH. She is frothing at the mouth. She will have your head, man. And guess who's getting the brunt of it every moment of every day?

TY. You are.

SETH. I am! I am getting raked over the coals because you knocked up her big sister and she is one pissed-off bride-to-be right now!

TY. What do you want me to say? Franny's pissed off? *Your* problem. Your problem is a lot smaller than my *problems.* Franny's annoying you? Guess what Seth? News Flash! Franny is an annoying little cooze! She was born that way! And I say this with all due respect, no offense.

SETH. None taken.

TY. Good. So I could care less as to how mad Franny is, okay? She wants my head, tell her to come and fucking take it. I don't use it anyway.

SETH. I'm just telling you, this is not small potatoes.

TY. Small what?

SETH. Potatoes.

TY. What?

SETH. Forget it. Look, with those other girls? That's your business, deal with them however you want. But I am connected to Jen, okay? She's going to be my sister-in-law.

TY. And I'm your best friend. Who's more important, Seth? Your future sister-in-law or your best friend since the first grade?

SETH. My future wife.

TY. Oh, you are a pussy. Oh my god, you are such a pussy.

SETH. All I'm saying is please *do something*.

TY. Like what?

SETH. Apologize! Start with that! Jen is freaked out, do you get that!? She tells you she's pregnant and you go crazy on her!? I mean the way she explains it, it was like she had turned into some giant mutant worm.

TY. I was freaking out!

SETH. It doesn't matter! She's a mess.

TY. So I apologize! Then what? What do I say? Jen, sweetheart, you should know you're not alone, I knocked up a couple more chicks while I was at it.

SETH. Tell her *something*.

TY. What? What do I say? How do I explain this?

SETH. I don't know. I don't know! *(Beat)* I DON'T KNOW!

Scene 8
Picture of Happiness

(Franny's kitchen.)

JEN. Just give me your blessing, okay?

FRANNY. Oh. You want a *blessing?* Fuck that. I'm not blessing shit. No bless. No bless from me.

JEN. Fine, don't bless.

FRANNY. I'm not.

JEN. Don't then.

FRANNY. Fine.

JEN. Fine.

(Beat)

FRANNY. *(Whines)* Jen...

JEN. *(Mock whines)* Franny...

FRANNY. I'm just saying. Why? Why *this particular...* *(She gestures to JEN's womb.)* The last thing you want is Ty's kid. His *offspring.*

JEN. It's how the cookie's crumbled.

FRANNY. Wrong! That's wrong and wrong-headed and you're doing this for the wrong reasons!

JEN. You don't know why—

FRANNY. —Defeatist. You're being defeatist.

JEN. No. I'm being optimistic. Life. Newness. Baby. Okay?

FRANNY. That's like the stupidest thing I've ever heard you say in my entire life. What about school?

JEN. What about it?

FRANNY. Jen, you're like the smartest person in the world. You have every degree known to man.

JEN. And? And what? What do I have to show for it? Why do you think I've been in school so long?

FRANNY. I don't know Jen. You love to read. You need therapy. Not a baby.

JEN. I'm embracing life!

FRANNY. Why don't you embrace my ass?

JEN. Franny... I understand that you want the best for me, but what I'd really like is to go eat. I want lunch. I want pad thai.

FRANNY. You're going to be *7 months pregnant* for my wedding. *Showing!*

JEN. So? I'll make you look skinny.

FRANNY. I—*What?*

JEN. What?

FRANNY. So I look *fat?*

JEN. That's not what I—

FRANNY. Oh that is low.

JEN. Fran, that's not—

FRANNY. Fine, go ahead! Get pregnant and get fat and be a fatty.

JEN. Fine! I will!

FRANNY. Fine!

(Beat)

FRANNY. You're gonna ruin my wedding pictures. What's it's going to be like? How is that going to feel to be all bloated up in front of everyone——in front of Grandma and Grandpa?

JEN. I can deal with it.

FRANNY. And what are you going to say when they ask you who the father is?

JEN. I don't know. I'll tell them it's the best man.

FRANNY. No you won't. If you think Ty is still Seth's best man, you're crazy.

JEN. Why, what happened now?

FRANNY. Ty just got uninvited to the wedding.

JEN. You can't do that. He's Seth's best friend.

FRANNY. I can do whatever I want. It's my wedding. Ty is OUT and Paco is IN.

JEN. Paco?

FRANNY. Seth's new best man. It was my idea.

JEN. He's ten years old!

FRANNY. He's twelve. And his English is getting better.

JEN. *Paco?*

FRANNY. He'll be adorable. He's a splash of color.

JEN. You're nuts.

FRANNY. But you... Jen, my big sis... I don't want you to be pregnant in my wedding pictures. We'll have to get your dress altered and you'll be huge and everything. I just don't want to have to explain you every time I show the pictures to someone.

JEN. What is your fixation with these wedding pictures?

FRANNY. It's not a fixation. It's—

JEN. Yes it is. Every time you open your mouth, you talk about your wedding pictures. You're obsessed or something. Stupid photographs.

FRANNY. They're not stupid. *(Beat)* Why would you say that? They're not stupid.

JEN. *Stupid.* Stupid *pictures.* No one ever looks at wedding pictures. You know why? They're stupid.

FRANNY. No! You're so negative! Anything that's important to me, you have to shit all over!

JEN. I'm looking for a little support and all you can talk
about is how I'm going to look in your stupid wedding pictures.

(Beat)

FRANNY. I have Mom and Dad's wedding pictures.

JEN. *What?*

FRANNY. Mom gave them to me.

JEN. Let me see them.

FRANNY. Mom gave them to me.

JEN. Even if they *did* have pictures Mom would have burned
them.

FRANNY. Well she didn't.

JEN. So let's see them.

FRANNY. Oh you want to *see* them?

JEN. Yeah.

FRANNY. Why? They're *stupid.* They're just stupid *pictures.*

JEN. There are no pictures. And Mom would never give you
something like that.

(FRANNY goes to a drawer and pulls a large photo out.)

FRANNY. Here it is.

JEN. One? One picture.

FRANNY. Mom and Dad on their wedding day. *(Looking at
it)* So happy. So full of hope.

JEN. Let me see it.
FRANNY. No.
JEN. Franny...
FRANNY. *(Mocking)* ... *Jen...*
JEN. *(Losing it) Let me see the fucking picture!*

(FRANNY hands JEN the picture.)

FRANNY. Here. Spaz. *(JEN looks at the picture. Long beat)* I know, right?
JEN. I mean... This is... *Look* at this. *(FRANNY and JEN look at the picture together.)* I can't believe you have this. Look at them.
FRANNY. I know.
JEN. I mean, Look at them, Fran.

(They look at the picture for a beat.)

FRANNY. I know.

(JEN puts the picture down.)

JEN. But it's folly, you know.
FRANNY. It's what?
JEN. Folly.
FRANNY. What the fuck is folly?
JEN. It's just—
FRANNY. What is that, like garnish at Christmas?
JEN. No, that's "Holly." Folly is—
FRANNY. No, forget it! I don't want to know. With your

stupid SAT words and everything. *(Mimicking JEN)* It's *Folly.* Fuck that! Fuck Folly.

JEN. All I'm saying is it's not real! It's just an image!

FRANNY. Oh, is that all?

JEN. Yes.

FRANNY. That's all your saying?

JEN. Jesus, Fran, yes.

FRANNY. Well, all *I'm* saying is you're going to be fat and bloated and ugly at my wedding and if I want to airbrush your fat stomach out of my wedding pictures I will!

Scene 9
The Precipice

(TY sits at a desk at school grading papers. BECCA enters.)

TY. Becca?

BECCA. Hi, Mr. Greene.

TY. Come on in. How's it going?

(BECCA sits down. She looks at him, takes a deep breath, nervous.)

BECCA. I'm sorry.

TY. For what?

BECCA. Everything.

TY. Everything.

BECCA. Yes. Look, you don't have to tell me anything, or like, comfort me. That's not why I'm here. I just wanted to apologize.

TY. Becca, what are you talking about?

BECCA. Look. Mr. Greene? I really—well you know I do—I really respect you.

TY. And I respect *you*.

BECCA. I mean, I've come here before. You've given me so much help and advice on how to be a poet and everything. And I really, I *really* appreciate it. I do. But I feel like I let you down.

TY. Becca... I really don't know what to say... Except that you're a brilliant student. And I have never.... I've always been thrilled to have you in my class.

BECCA. It was a stupid poem.

TY. Your poem... Today? That poem?

BECCA. You don't have to be nice to me. I can take it.

TY. Becca, you put your soul into that poem.

BECCA. Whatev. If that's what my soul sounds like, then I'm in trouble.

TY. What was it called again?

BECCA. "The Precipice."

TY. "The Precipice." Let me see it.

BECCA. Now?

TY. Yeah, now. *(BECCA goes to her bag and pulls out a piece of paper that is crumpled up into a ball.)* Well, this isn't very nice, is it? This isn't a nice way to treat a poem at all.

BECCA. Whatev.

TY. Let me take another look at it, okay? *(TY smoothens it out and reads from it.)*

"I am standing on the precipice of my life..."
    Okay, that's a good start. I know where you are. I know
what's going on with you. Okay?
    BECCA. Okay.
    TY.
"And the wind blows.
And life is such a confusion."
    Good. Nice images. You're very focused, do you know that?
    BECCA. I am?
    TY. You're a very focused poet. As a *person*, well, none of
us poets are very focused as *people* are we?
    BECCA. I guess not.
    TY. That's why we write poetry.
    BECCA. Why?
    TY. Because we're unfocused.
    BECCA. Oh, right.
    TY. There's a rhythm to this. An insistence. You're search-
ing for something.
    BECCA. What?
    TY. I don't know. You tell me.
    BECCA. Tell you what?
    TY. What are you searching for? *(Beat)* In the poem...
    BECCA. I don't know.
    TY. Exactly. That's why this poem is working.
    BECCA. Right.
    TY.
"Why do I wait for the stallion that does not ride?"
    Okay, the stallion. What is the stallion, exactly?
    BECCA. It's a kind of horse.
    TY. No, I know. I mean, what does the stallion represent

here? *(BECCA thinks.)* We'll come back to that.
"Why do I stand upon the edge with such wind around me?
What if I fall?
And now I am falling."
　　Nice repetition.
"Stars and sky and wind and moon. Oh Blackness!
Around me all is blackness, except for stars and moon.
Stars and moon, which are whiteness.
All else which is blackness..."
　　I like the contrast. Black and white. We're dealing with extremes. There's no gray here is there?
　　BECCA. No, nothing is gray.
　　TY. I know. Nothing is. Everything is either something or nothing.
　　BECCA. I mean, that was like a poem, what you just said.
　　TY. Nah.
　　BECCA. No, it was. Everything you say is like a poem.
　　TY.
"And then impact!
Where have I fallen?
My heart sinks and rises at the same time when I see where I am...
I am on the precipice.
The precipice of my life."
　　(BECCA and TY look at each other.) I don't want you going around thinking you can't write poetry. I don't want you crumpling these things up. I want you to trust yourself a little bit more. We need poems like these, Becca.
　　BECCA. I don't really know what to say to that.
　　TY. Well, it's the truth.
　　BECCA. Mr. Greene?

TY. *Ty.*
BECCA. Ty?
TY. What?
BECCA. I probably shouldn't tell you this.
TY. What?
BECCA. Your book, *Labyrinth*? I mean, you know I've read it. I mean, you assigned it, so I had to... but, I've never really told you... I think it's... I just think it's kind of remarkable.
TY. Wow. Thank you Becca.
BECCA. I mean... they're not like my poems. My poems are so emo and everything. Your poems are so not emo.
TY. Well thank you, Becca. I'm not sure what "emo" means, but thank you.

(They smile at each other.)

BECCA. You're funny.
TY. No, I'm serious. I don't know what "emo" means.
BECCA. Ha! Okay. I guess I should go.
TY. Okay. Well, keep writing.
BECCA. I will. *(BECCA gets up and goes to leave, but stops and turns to TY.)* Ty?
TY. Yeah?
BECCA. Thanks. I'm sorry I'm such a mess.
TY. It's okay. It's okay to be a mess.

Scene 10
Best Man

(Back at Ty's apartment.)

SETH. You're lucky she is actually 18, you know that?

TY. There's nothing you can tell me that I am not thinking at every moment. I *regret* it, okay? I regretted it before I found out she was pregnant.

SETH. I'm not telling Franny about this. Or Jen. Franny will burst into flames if she hears this shit.

TY. Well, eventually she's going to find out. Right?

SETH. What are you going to do?

TY. I don't know.

(Beat)

SETH. I have to go.

TY. Look. I'll talk to Jen. At some point.

SETH. I know. *(SETH turns to go.)* Oh. Shit. There's one other thing.

TY. What.

SETH. This is... this is just one of those things.

TY. What?

SETH. Franny doesn't want you in the wedding.

TY. What?

SETH. She told me. It's like one of her demands all of a sudden. You can't be in the wedding.

TY. I'm your *Best Man*!

SETH. I know.

TY. Are you kidding me?

SETH. Look, I'm trying.

TY. What do you mean you're trying?

SETH. To get you an invitation. I mean, I still want you there. But the whole Best Man thing... It would be better if you just let that go for now.

TY. *Let it go?*

SETH. I know, I'm sorry, but you know Franny. There's no way she's going to let you be in the wedding party.

TY. She has no say! She has no fucking say!

SETH. She does. You know how girls are about their weddings. She's carrying on and on about *wedding pictures*.

TY. So who's gonna be your best man?

SETH. Paco.

TY. *Paco!?*

SETH. Yeah.

TY. He's twelve years old!

SETH. He's thirteen.

TY. *Paco?!* Little Paco is your best man!?

SETH. Yeah.

TY. You *tutor* him! You're his *tutor!*

SETH. Three times a week.

TY. He doesn't speak *English!*

SETH. No, he's gotten better. He's a sweet kid.

TY. He's got *Down's Syndrome!*

SETH. So?

TY. He's a tiny Mexican kid with Down's Syndrome!

SETH. Whoa! Hold on there, Ty. That's out of line. He's Venezuelan.

TY. Best friends since the first grade and you're booting me from your wedding party because you can't stand up to your wench of a fiancée.

SETH. Look it's not about standing up to her. It's the wedding thing. She's crazy enough about... everything... but this wedding thing, man, I stay out of her way, you know? She's on a rampage.

TY. I hate her.

SETH. I know. But it's just for the time being. Things will mellow as time passes.

TY. Seth, if this goes down—if I am expelled from your wedding, from being your best man, there *is* no going back. It's like Franny saying, "Ty is out of the picture. He's not our friend." It's over between us if this happens. Don't you see that?

SETH. You're being dramatic.

TY. Every other person in the world is about to walk out on me. I need to know you won't. Tell me you have faith in me. I need it. Your faith. I need it right now.

SETH. Why didn't you just stay together with Jen in the first place? You guys were a good couple.

(Beat)

TY. I don't know.

SETH. She loves you, man. She's really... She would marry you right now if you asked her.

TY. I know.

SETH. So?

TY. I don't want to marry her.

SETH. You don't love her.

TY. Come on, man.

SETH. Do you love Maureen or Becca?

TY. No.

SETH. Well, shit. You know, most men would flip over backwards to get Jen, you know that.

TY. Yeah.

SETH. She's hot.

TY. I know.

SETH. She's hotter than Franny and nicer, too. *(TY looks at SETH.)* I'm just saying...

TY. I know, okay?

SETH. I wish you weren't such a fuck up. We could have been brothers-in-law. *(Beat)* I'll call you.

(SETH leaves.)

Scene 11
Two Years Earlier

(TY stands holding a notebook and a plastic cup of wine at reception after a poetry reading. JEN, FRANNY and SETH enter. Also with plastic cups.)

FRANNY. There he is! There he is! The big star!

SETH. Dude that was awesome! That kid's like: I'm making a Labyrinth! Outta nothing!

TY. Hey, thanks for coming you guys.

FRANNY. Ty, this is my sister *Jen.*

TY. Oh my God! I've heard so much... so much about you...

JEN. Hi. Me too. Nice to finally—

FRANNY. —That was so cool! I can't believe you could read like that in front of the whole people like that, the whole crowd!

TY. How's the wine, Franny?

SETH. She's wasted.

FRANNY. I am *not.*

SETH. *Wasted.*

FRANNY. But I tell you what: I am going to *get* wasted. Yes I am. These glasses are like shot glasses cups. Shot cups.

TY. *(To JEN)* So you're in that MFA program, right? Poetry?

FRANNY. *(Stating obvious)* Poet... Poet...

JEN. Um. Yeah. I mean, I was. I just graduated.

FRANNY. Well we're going to go get some more wine and it'll probably take a LONG TIME because of I have to pee. So Okay!

(FRANNY starts to exit. SETH stays with TY, oblivious.)

SETH. Ya know Labyrinth is from the Greek.

FRANNY. *Seth...*

SETH. Oh! Oh, okay. Wine. We'll both get wine!

(They start to leave.)

FRANNY. *(Whisper)* ...So dense sometimes!

SETH. *(Whisper)* Sorry!

(They exit. TY and JEN smile at each other.)

TY. Hi.

JEN. That was really great.

TY. Oh, thanks.

JEN. Really great.

TY. Thanks.

JEN. Jeez, I'm sorry. What a stupid... what a stupid thing to say.

TY. No.

JEN. "Really great." How poetic.

TY. Trust me, I'll take what I can get. I mean truth be told, I'm just a dork with a notebook. I haven't published anything or anything.

JEN. Oh, you will.

TY. Nah.

JEN. No, you will!

TY. Have you?

JEN. Published? Oh no way. Not quite. I quit writing poetry. Tonight I quit.

TY. Why?

JEN. I like to quit things. I quit being a lawyer, too.

TY. That's right! Franny told me! You're a lawyer!

JEN. Never took the bar. Went from undergrad to law school to the MFA program...

TY. You're a lawyer poet!

JEN. Poetic Counsel.

TY. What do you do now that you're not lawyering or writing poetry?

JEN. I'm in a doctoral program.

TY. *Higher* education!

JEN. I just really love school.

TY. So you're like super smart.

JEN. Oh yeah. *Super* smart.

TY. How poetic... What's your *dissertation* about?

JEN. Geography. You ever hear of Pangaea?

TY. The one big continent.

JEN. I'm drawing a better map of it. That's my dissertation.

TY. You're mapping a non-existent place.

JEN. In way, it still exists. It's the world. Now, it's just broken up into pieces. Once upon a time, we looked different.

TY. The adolescent earth.

JEN. It was the Garden of Eden you know. One piece of land. Perfect. Untouched. *(They both smile at each other, but JEN breaks the spell.)* Ha! *(Giggles)* I'm sorry. I've had like ten little cups of wine.

TY. *Little* cups.

JEN. Yes, they are little.

TY. And free.

JEN. My favorite kind of wine.

TY. Always a good year.

JEN. Yes. The year free. Two thousand free.

TY. Cheers. *(Beat)* Yeah. I liked... I liked watching you read.

(JEN kisses him, not too long, not too short. They look at each other, smile. Drink their wine.)

Scene 12
Flesh and Blood

(MAUREEN and TY on the porch.)

MAUREEN. Do you sleep with a lot of women?
TY. What?
MAUREEN. Do you?
TY. No! What do you think?
MAUREEN. I think you might.
TY. Do *you*? I mean, have you ever... before?
MAUREEN. No. Me and Nick... I mean, our relationship is different.
TY. But you still love him?

(Beat)

MAUREEN. You know, I can't... I can't *conceive.*
TY . You can't have kids? What about Augie?
MAUREEN. He was adopted.
TY. Right. Wow. Sorry. Kids.
MAUREEN. You think about your kids your whole life, before they even exist, you think about them. You plan who they'll be. You think about what they'll look like. And then... It doesn't work out the way you planned. *(Beat)* I wanted to feel that, you know? I imagine it's about as religious an experience as one can come by. Miraculous. How many things happen to you that are *miraculous*?
TY. I don't know. I mean, the whole world is miraculous

when you think about it.

MAUREEN. Are you religious?

TY. Me? No. Are you?

MAUREEN. No. I'm Catholic.

TY. Really?

MAUREEN. Raised. Lapsed. *(Beat)* I believe in sin.

TY. Well... *yeah.* There's no denying that.

MAUREEN. I mean, I believe in Original Sin. That we need to seek forgiveness and work towards our salvation... which is really a messed up belief to have when you've stopped believing in God.

TY. Are you an atheist?

MAUREEN. I'm worse. I'm atheist who's still pissed off at God for not existing. It's a stressful denomination.

TY. I'd say.

MAUREEN. You're supposed to have faith even if your prayers aren't answered. All I wanted was to give birth, have a child. It's the only thing I ever explicitly asked God for. When I found out it couldn't happen... well that was the end of that.

TY. Do you think what we're doing is a sin?

MAUREEN. Oh yes. But it's a sin I can sink my teeth into.

(Beat)

MAUREEN. Do you have anyone else?

TY. No.

MAUREEN. I don't care if you do, but... I was being foolish. We're *being* foolish. I just want to know, okay?

TY. I haven't had sex with anyone else in a long time.

Scene 13
Growing as a Poet

(TY opens his front door and BECCA enters.)

BECCA. Hi!

TY. Hey there! What a surprise to get your call!

BECCA. I mean was in the neighborhood? I was having brunch. I totally love Brooklyn. It's so retro.

TY. Yeah, it is. So... here you are.

BECCA. I hope I'm not intruding...

TY. No! I was just writing.

BECCA. Wow. Of course. *(She pulls out wine.)* I brought some wine.

TY. Wine!

BECCA. Because my new poem? It's about wine.

TY. Oh. That's good... good material... Well, come on in. Make yourself at home...

BECCA. Awesome! This place is so cool! It's like a writer's lair.

TY. Yep. It is.

BECCA. So are you writing a new book of poetry?

TY. Uh, Yes. That's what I'm trying to do...

BECCA. Is it going to be like *Labyrinth*?

TY. Well, I hope not *too* much like Labyrinth. I mean, I hope I'm growing as a poet.

BECCA. I can't believe you're going to *grow* as a poet.

TY. The things that concern you change. The things that inspire you change.

BECCA. What inspired you for *Labyrinth*?

TY. A woman.

BECCA. Oooh. A woman. Who?

TY. This was years ago, you know. Like four years ago.

BECCA. Yeah?

TY. I was in love with her. But she left me for another man who she then married.

BECCA. Oh, wow. I'm so sorry.

TY. Sometimes relationships end. But you always have that distant hope they might begin again... but when someone gets married, then it's a whole different story. Marriage is so final.

BECCA. Yeah. I know. Except for, like, divorce.

TY. So I wrote about it. People like it.

BECCA. People love it.

TY. I don't know. Big picture is, nobody really reads poetry. I'll never sell large amounts of books.

BECCA. It doesn't matter how many you sell. If your poetry affects one person, then that's all that matters. That's how you change the world. You're changing the world with your poetry.

TY. *(To audience)* Are you kidding me? You hear something like that out of a beautiful girl's mouth? What are you going to think? I'll tell you what you're *not* going to think: You're *not* going to think, *she's just a dumb lovesick girl who's just flattering me.* You're thinking: *My poetry is changing the world.*

BECCA. *(To TY)* I mean, you're an artist. That's what you do.

TY. *(To audience) I mean, I'm an artist. That's what I do. (Beat. TY turns back to BECCA. To BECCA)* That's a little much.

BECCA. No, I mean it.

TY. Well thank you. Thank you, Becca.

(BECCA sees MAUREEN's kid's ball.)

    BECCA. Oh, wow! What an awesome ball!
    TY. That? Yeah, that's just a.... it's a cool ball.
    BECCA. Where did you get this?
    TY. It's actually the kid next door's.
    BECCA. Why do you have it?
    TY. I play with him sometimes. You know, like babysit. I
like kids.
    BECCA. That's so sweet.

*(She smiles at him. He smiles back. She throws the ball at him.
He catches it and tosses it back. She throws it back and they
play catch, slowly closing the space between them. BECCA
tosses the ball aside and kisses TY. TY starts kissing back.
They start making out.)*

    TY. I'll go get a condom...
    BECCA. I'm on the pill.

(TY stares at her for a beat.)

    TY. I'll go get a condom.

(BECCA pulls him to her body.)

    BECCA. It's okay. It's good.

(TY goes with it.)

Scene 14
Something Immaculate

(Spotlight on MAUREEN.)

MAUREEN. I am not supposed to be able to do this. I'm not. This is pretty much impossible. And so... when the impossible becomes real... Something Immaculate. I'm pregnant, Ty. You've made me pregnant.

(TY appears.)

TY. How do you know Nick isn't the father?

MAUREEN. Nick and I haven't had sex in a year.

TY. In a year! In a year. You told me you couldn't get pregnant!

MAUREEN. I believed I couldn't. That's supposed to be the truth about... about me. The scientific truth. But it's not. There's something deeper.

TY. What are you going to do?

MAUREEN. I haven't thought it through yet, but I wanted you to be the first to know. I wanted to... thank you. Somehow you've given me the one thing I've always wanted in the world. And not only that, Ty: My faith. In God, I mean. I'm serious. I'm filled with.... so much right now...

TY. *(Desperate)* How did you get pregnant!?

MAUREEN. I'm telling you it was a miracle.

TY. Miracles don't happen.

MAUREEN. They happen all the time. This time, one happened to me.

TY. So you're going to keep it?

MAUREEN. *Keep* it?

TY. Sorry...

MAUREEN. This is a spiritual thing. This is... *God.* And me. And a child.

TY. Don't say that.

MAUREEN. I love you.

TY. Don't say *that*!

MAUREEN. I don't want anything from you Ty. I don't expect you to do anything. But I am so filled with... I don't know! The Holy Spirit!

TY. You're not filled with the Holy Spirit!

MAUREEN. I am! I am and I've never felt so complete!

(MAUREEN exits. A spotlight up on BECCA on her cell phone.)

TY'S VOICE. Hi, this is Ty. Leave a message.

WOMAN'S VOICE. At the tone, please leave a message. When you are finished, you may hang up, or press pound for more options. To leave a call back number, press 1. *(Beat)* To page this person press 5.

(A beep)

BECCA. Hey, Ty, this is Becca. Hey. Um, look, this is kind of awkward? But I... and I'm not trying to be weird or anything, or like stalkerish here? I'm really not, but we should probably talk sometime? Because... Well, here's the thing? I'm pregnant? So... that's some news. And I don't want you to freak out or anything, because it's really not that big of a deal? I mean, it is, but I'm not going to be some crazy girl about this whole thing, so you can relax about that. I'm just kind of curious what your take is on all this, and maybe if you have any strong opinions about... anything. Um, so cool? Okay. Thanks. I... I uh... Okay cool.

(She hangs up. Exits. JEN enters.)

    TY. That's impossible.
    JEN. No. It's not.
    TY. Not from me.
    JEN. Yes! Ty! From you!
    TY. This is a joke.
    JEN. No. Ty, listen. Will you listen?
    TY. Tell me this some stupid sick joke! Tell me that!
    JEN. What's wrong with you?!
    TY. Tell me that!
    JEN. Shut up!
    TY. This is some stupid sick fucking joke! Tell me! Tell me that now!
    JEN. Stop it! Stop it!
    TY. Why are you doing this to me!
    JEN. Ty, stop it! What's wrong with you?

(TY paces, angry, freaking out.)

    TY. We used a condom!
    JEN. It broke!
    TY. No it didn't!

JEN. It must have!

TY. But it didn't, Jen! It didn't break! It didn't fucking break!

JEN. Well, one way or the other, Ty... IT DIDN'T WORK!

Scene 15
Making Something Messy

(TY stands center, speaks to the audience. As he speaks, he puts on an apron.)

TY. So I'm having Seth and Franny and Jen over for dinner. It was this sort of unspoken deal that I hashed out with Seth. Have them and Jen over for dinner. A peace offering. A "we're all friends" sort of thing, and then presto, All Will Be Forgiven. But here's the thing. I'm a little fucked up in the head these days and I know things are going to go horribly wrong tonight. I know this because Maureen caught me on the porch today and said she'd like to talk sometime and I said, "Oh, okay, how about tonight? Come over. I'll make dinner." Meanwhile, Becca also wants to chat. I told her to stop by when she's free and I know for a fact that she's free tonight.

And so I'm pretty sure all of these women are going to converge here tonight where they will all meet and all come to the problematic realization that within each of them grows my unbelievably potent seed. *(Beat)* I cook. Chicks dig it. Tonight I'm making something a little messy, but I like to experiment and see if it'll be just right. For the occasion. Anyhow, I'm cooking here, and I'm remembering this thing from when I was a kid. I was like 5 years old and I was sitting at the dinner table and I had a bowl of peas and carrots in front of me and my father was standing over me demanding that I eat the peas and carrots. I refused. He yelled at me and threatened me and I began to cry, but I stared him down, tears running down my face, a tight scowl across my mouth. My father got angrier and he pointed at me and yelled, "You eat those vegetables NOW or we're going to have a BIG problem, Mister!" And, staring at him, I put my little hand under the bowl and I flipped it up in the air. Peas and carrots everywhere. Holy shit.

(The doorbell rings.)

ACT II

Scene 16
In a Pickle

(TY stands far to the side of the stage while JEN, MAUREEN, and BECCA stand facing the audience. They speak out at the audience.)

TY. *(To audience)* So I told them and at first, they were like... *(The women stand in shock. To audience)* And *then* they were like:

MAUREEN. How could you do this! I'm asking! Look at me! Look at me when I'm talking to you! How irresponsible and dangerous and what is wrong with you? You just go around fucking every woman you see? Is that it? Notches on your belt? Notches, Ty?

JEN. No. You're... No. Ty... Just... just... What are you doing? Why are we all here at the same time together!? What is WRONG with you? What has been missing from your life that you have to be so... *Who are you?*

BECCA. I had no idea you got so much action. *(Beat)* I mean, I'm serious... *(Beat)* I mean: Whoa.

(FRANNY enters quickly, looking out at the audience.)

FRANNY. Stupid cocksucking piece of shit.
TY. *(To audience)* So that's pretty much what they were like.
Except they were all talking at the same time. Look, I'm sorry.
It's hard to remember how it all went down. It was a blur. I mean
I remember, what they all looked like and the kind of appalling,
horrific tension that quickly spread through the apartment like
wildfire. But it's hard to remember it perfectly. How it all went
down. For example it really sounded more like: *(A hellish
screaming of female demons from the depths of hell is briefly
heard. To audience)* And here's the thing: I wanted this. I wanted
everyone to converge. I needed it to happen. I mean, breaking
this kind of news to a girl... THREE TIMES... and having to
deal with the fallout three times and I'm telling you: I just could-
n't handle that. I'm weak. So... Dinner. Everyone at once. Three
birds with one stone.

Scene 17
Dinner

(Doorbell rings. Bowl of pickles is on the coffee table.)

TY. Come in! *(SETH enters.)* Yo.
SETH. Yo.
TY. Hungry?
SETH. Listen.
TY. What?

SETH. What's going on tonight?

TY. What do you mean?

SETH. What's the plan?

TY. Dinner's the plan. Where's Franny and Jen?

SETH. Listen.

TY. *What?*

SETH. So I got you back in the wedding.

TY. You did?

SETH. At least for now.

TY. Holy shit. You did it!

SETH. Well…

TY. I love you.

SETH. Shut up.

TY. Best Friend! Best Man!

SETH. Listen.

TY. *What?*

SETH. I lied about you.

TY. What do you mean?

SETH. Okay. Bear with me. Franny thinks you're going to propose to Jen.

(TY stares at SETH.)

TY. You *told* her this? *(SETH shrugs.)* You told Franny I was going to *propose?* To *Jen?*

SETH. I had to tell her something!

TY. Why?!

SETH. I'm sorry! You don't have to do it *tonight.* But she thinks you might do it. *(Looks at the coffee table)* Are these pickles?

TY. You just LIED?

SETH. I had to tell Franny something. You know?

TY. No, Seth, I don't know. I don't fucking know.

SETH. She gets in my head! And if I want her to give in on something, I've got to feed her. I've got to have something to give her. You know, like concessions. Collateral. I don't know.

TY. You are the biggest douche bag I've ever met in my life.

SETH. But when I start telling her shit, I don't know, it's like the way she stares at me or something. It's hypnotic, but I actually start to believe what I'm saying.

(Doorbell rings.)

TY. Well, I'm not. I'm not going to propose! Jesus! Will you get that?

(SETH answers door. FRANNY enters.)

SETH. Hey honey!

FRANNY. What a fucking day. So I'm in this— *(They kiss.)* Hi sweetie... So I'm in this meeting this afternoon and that slut Beverly takes the proposal I've been working on with Jack and she flips it across the conference table, in front of everyone, and she's like, "What can I do with this?" What can I do with this? And of course, Jack wasn't there. She never would have done that if Jack were there, but no. *What can I fucking do with this?*

SETH. Heh.

FRANNY. Exactly. *(Looks at TY)* Well. There he is. *Daddy.*

TY. Hi Fran.

(FRANNY gives him a box of condoms.)

FRANNY. Mazel Tov! These are what they call "Condoms." There's directions inside.

TY. Aw. You shouldn't have.

FRANNY. And here's some beer.

TY. Condoms and beer. You're my type of girl, Franny.

FRANNY. Don't get cute. You're lucky I don't slit your fucking throat right now, the way you treated Jen. I need a cigarette.

TY. Well you're here now. And we're all friends.

FRANNY. *(Fake sing-songy)* Yes we are! Yes we are, Ty! *(Normal)* By the way, I have a contact list *this long* if you want. All the people you'll need for the wedding, all ready to go. I'll email it.

SETH. Sweetie! We don't need to talk about that yet!

FRANNY. *(To SETH)* Well, I mean—

TY. I'm gonna put these in the fridge. You guys?

FRANNY & SETH. Yeah.

(TY hands them two beers and exits.)

FRANNY. *(After TY)* And I'm serious, Ty! I have a threshold.

SETH. Franny! Hi! Why don't we sit down...

FRANNY. I'm just saying! She's gonna be... *(She pantomimes huge pregnant/bloated.)* Weddings don't happen overnight. I'm so glad we're not like them.

SETH. Yeah.

FRANNY. How was your day, sweetie?

SETH. It was... fine, listen, there's something I should—

FRANNY. What are these pickles? Gross.

(TY enters.)

TY. Dinner should be ready in about a half hour.

FRANNY. God I'm starving. *(To SETH)* Sweetie, will you go get me cigarettes?

TY. I thought you quit.

FRANNY. I did. That's why I don't have any. Sweetie?

SETH. Weren't you just *at* the store? *(FRANNY just looks at SETH.)* Ty, you need anything?

TY. Nope.

SETH. Cool. Be right back.

(SETH exits. TY and FRANNY look at each other.)

TY. So. *(Beat)* So how are thi—

FRANNY. —So I can't say I'm *thrilled* at the prospect of having you as a *brother-in-law...(TY shakes his head, laughing.)* No, I'm serious.

TY. *(Marveling at her)* Franny.

FRANNY. *(Mimic)* Ty.

TY. *(Quiet)* Franny.

FRANNY. *(Mimic)* Ty. *(Beat. They stare at each other. The doorbell rings. Excited; gets up)* There she is!

(FRANNY hums "Here Comes the Bride." TY exits to kitchen. FRANNY gets the door. BECCA is there.)

FRANNY. Um... Yeah?

BECCA. Hi.

FRANNY. Hi.

BECCA. Is Ty here?

FRANNY. He's busy. Can I help you?

BECCA. I'm here for dinner...I didn't know anyone else was going to be here. I thought it was...

FRANNY. You're here for dinner.

BECCA. He told me to come over. We had some stuff to...

(TY enters.)

TY. Becca! Come on in. You guys met.

FRANNY. Actually, no.

TY. Well this is Becca, she's my student and this is—

FRANNY. —This is your *student?*

BECCA. Am I like really early?

TY. No. This is good. You guys make yourselves comfortable... Drink?

FRANNY. Ty, what's going on here?

TY. What do you mean?

FRANNY. —I mean, this was supposed to be a private dinner...

TY. Is this your dinner party, Fran?

FRANNY. No, but—

TY. No, So just shut up and relax. Becca you want a drink? You want a beer?

BECCA. Do you have club soda with a lime?

TY. You got it. I'll be back in a jiffy.

(TY exits. FRANNY, clearly pissed off, sits down. BECCA goes

sits across from her. They look at each other.)

BECCA. So how do you know Ty?
FRANNY. My sister.
BECCA. Oh. He's your sister?
FRANNY. *What?*
BECCA. I'm kidding!
FRANNY. So you're Ty's student.
BECCA. Yeah. I'm in his poetry workshop. It's pretty rad.
FRANNY. I bet it is.
BECCA. Wow, I love your shoes!
FRANNY. These?
BECCA. They're like super classy but still kind of casual.
FRANNY. Yeah, they're not really casual at all.
BECCA. Oh, then I take it back. Those shoes suck.
FRANNY. What year are you?
BECCA. I'm a first year.
FRANNY. You're a *freshman?*
BECCA. Yeah, I'm a first year.
FRANNY. So you're like… really young.
BECCA. I mean, yeah. Comparatively.

(FRANNY's brain explodes. SETH enters.)

SETH. I got smokes. And I got some muthafuckin turkey jerkey! *(He turns and sees BECCA.)* Whoa.
FRANNY. *(To SETH)* Do you know about this? About *Becca?*
SETH. About what? I don't know! What do I know? I got smokes and they had, I got some, you know…. *What?* Hi, I'm

Seth.

FRANNY. She's here for *dinner*. She's Ty's *student*.

BECCA. I'm sorry it's so weird that I'm here. I mean, Ty invited me and everything.

SETH. You're Becca! Oh wow! That's great! And you're here for for for dinner!

BECCA. Ty invited me. He called me up today and invited me. Who are you?

FRANNY. He's my fiancé.

BECCA. Wow, you guys are like *married* and everything.

FRANNY. *(To SETH)* She's a *freshman*.

SETH. *(To BECCA)* Yeah! I loved school! I was a great student, I mean, I think I had like a 3.8 cumulative average. Was it a 3.8 honey? I think it was a 3.8 I was like a major nerd back then. School. School was nice. Are you having a good... How's school?

BECCA. It's pretty—

SETH. Do you like Turkey Jerkey? Have some?

FRANNY. Can I have my fucking cigarettes?

(SETH gives her a pack. FRANNY whacks it against her palm repeatedly, looking menacingly from SETH to BECCA.)

BECCA. Wow, you smoke?

FRANNY. Uh. Yeah.

BECCA. I read this article about smokers mouths? I mean everyone knows smoking is bad and everything, but people who smoke, they have like these microscopic... *wounds*... all over the insides of their mouths that *never go away*. Even if you quit.

SETH. You know what's awesome? You know what's really

cool? Where's Ty? Ty? *(Shouts desperately) TY!*

(TY enters from kitchen.)

TY, Yo!

(SETH walks so the girls can't see him and gestures madly to TY, freaking out.)

FRANNY. *(To TY)* So Ty! Are your other students coming over for dinner tonight? Or just this one?
SETH. Oh! You know what? I think I just remembered that I left the stove on at our place?
FRANNY. What?
SETH. The stove! The freaking stove! We gotta go. Fran, we should probably—

(The doorbell rings.)

FRANNY. Finally!

(FRANNY opens the door. MAUREEN's there.)

MAUREEN. Hi...

(FRANNY just walks away.)

FRANNY. Jesus F-ing Christ! What *is* this?

(MAUREEN walks in, uncertain. FRANNY starts smoking.)

MAUREEN. Hi? Ty? I'm sorry... you said tonight, right?

(TY walks up to her.)

TY. Of course! Maureen. Welcome. Hi.

(MAUREEN kisses him.)

SETH. *(Re: the kiss)* Whoa. Hey, you know what? Maybe me and Franny should... I mean... HA! Hi everyone!
TY. No, I'm sorry I wasn't clear to everyone... this is like a dinner party! Everyone here. All my friends! It's a celebra—It's a gathering. Everyone, this is Maureen, she's my next door neighbor. This is Seth, Franny, and Becca.
MAUREEN. Hello...
BECCA. I love that shirt!
MAUREEN. Oh! Thank you! It's Old Navy.
TY. Can I get you a drink?
MAUREEN. I don't know... club soda?
TY. Sure. *(He starts to exit.)* There's some pickles there...
MAUREEN. *(Goes to them)* Ooh!

(He exits. MAUREEN eats pickles.)

MAUREEN. Ty always has the best pickles.
FRANNY. So you're his neighbor.
SETH. Neighbor... neighborly... neighborly...
MAUREEN. Um... I'm sorry... But could you not smoke?
FRANNY. Could I not smoke?
BECCA. It gives you mouth wounds.

MAUREEN. I'm sorry. It's just...
FRANNY. *(Stubbing out)* No! Fine! I won't smoke!

(Uncomfortable beat)

SETH. Smoking indoors! What is this, the Midwest?
MAUREEN. So how do you guys know Ty?
FRANNY. Well, she's like his student or something. She's a freshman, I'm sorry, a "First Year" and she's... what are you 16?
BECCA. I'm 14 and a half.
FRANNY. Yeah and she's like really *cute.* And I'm here because my sister is coming and she and Ty are like... you know, she's with him.

(Beat)

MAUREEN. Wait... what?
FRANNY. Ty's with my sister?
MAUREEN. I'm sorry?
SETH. And what do you do, Maureen?
BECCA. Ty has a girlfriend?
FRANNY. She's going to be here any second. Her name is Jen.
MAUREEN. And she's...? Your sister.
FRANNY. She's with Ty.
MAUREEN. She's *with* Ty.
BECCA. That's a little vague ya know. I mean when some- one is with someone...
SETH. You know what game I like? Pictionary. That game rocks. Ty has it. I'll get it. *(Exiting to kitchen)* Ty?! Where's your

god damn Pictionary?!

(SETH exits to kitchen.)

    MAUREEN. Wait a minute. Your sister...
    FRANNY. Jen.
    SETH. *(Offstage; muted)* What is *HAPPENING!?*
    MAUREEN. She and Ty...
    FRANNY. She's with him.
    BECCA. What does that even *mean?*
    MAUREEN. Yeah, what does that mean?
    FRANNY. She's with him! Why is this so confusing? She's
like with him!

(MAUREEN thinks.)

    MAUREEN. You know what? I gotta go.

(She heads for the door.)

    FRANNY. Why? How do you know him?
    MAUREEN. We've been... I've been cheating on my hus-
band with Ty for the last few months. So tell your sister that.
    FRANNY. Oh shit. Oh shit, I will.

*(Doorbell rings. MAUREEN opens it. JEN rushes in with back-
pack and bicycle helmet.)*

    JEN. Hi! *(She stops, looks around, surprised at all the peo-
ple.)* Hi, I have to pee.

(JEN rushes into the bathroom, slams the door. SETH and TY enter from kitchen. Everyone looks at them. SETH has Pictionary.)

SETH. Who's up for some Pictionary?

(The sound of JEN throwing up comes from the bathroom. Everyone listens. Flush. Running water. Rinsing mouth. Clearing flem. The whole bit. JEN enters from bathroom.)

JEN. Hi. Sorry. I had to pee. *(Beat; goes to coffee table)* Ooh, are those pickles?
MAUREEN. *(To TY)* You're a son of a bitch.
TY. Yeah?
MAUREEN. You could have just told me the truth.
JEN. What?
FRANNY. Ty's been fucking her.
JEN. *What?*
FRANNY. And maybe kiddie porn over there, too.
TY. Hey, Franny, you know, shut up.
BECCA. Whoa. This is wack.
FRANNY. No! Is that it too? Are you fucking your neighbor AND your student, Ty? This nubile little freshmen who isn't old enough to drink?
BECCA. I am not nubile!
MAUREEN. I can't believe this...
JEN. Oh...
TY. Jen...
BECCA. That is so uncalled for. Like I'm some sort of nubile pariah. I'm going Ty, I'll call you.

(JEN runs for the door.)

MAUREEN. Jesus, Ty...
TY. Wait! Just wait! It's worse than you think! *(Beat; to audience)* So I told them. *(The women stop, look at him. Lights shift. To audience)* And I will admit to something strange and perhaps very fucked up. There was a sense of the sublime in all this. The thrill of being caught, the thrill of having done something unbelievable, something that puts me in a very bad light. It was a rush. Terrifying, but also amazing. All these hysterical women, shocked, angry. Their anger a hot blue, a whiteness. The way fire looks almost cold when it is the hottest it can get. And then...
BECCA. Okay, so I'm like due back on the planet earth? You guys take care. I'm out.

(BECCA exits.)

MAUREEN. I cannot believe this. YOU are sick, Ty. I can't believe that you're part of... That you... Jesus Mary and Joseph.

(MAUREEN exits. JEN sits against the wall. FRANNY lunges at TY to kill him. SETH jumps in, puts her in a half nelson and struggles to keep her away from TY.)

FRANNY. I'll fucking kill you! Do you understand me! I will end your miserable little life, Ty!
TY. Jen.... Jen look at me...
FRANNY. Jen! You are coming with us! I will not leave you

with this... this...
    JEN. Franny.
    FRANNY. Come on!
    JEN. I need to be alone with Ty for a second.
    FRANNY. Fuck that!
    SETH. We gotta go.
    JEN. Wait for me outside.
    FRANNY. *(To TY)* If she's not out in five minutes I am coming back and I will kill you for real.

(SETH ushers her out the door.)

    SETH. I'll call you dude...
    FRANNY. *(Offstage)* This isn't done! Ty, this isn't done!
    TY. Look... This wasn't supposed to... *(JEN starts crying.)* Aw Jesus. Jen? Lemme get you some club soda or something.

(He goes to get a drink, JEN stands up, suddenly stronger.)

    JEN. No! Fuck you.
    TY. Jen...
    JEN. Why would you do this?
    TY. Do... what?
    JEN. DO *WHAT!?*
    TY. I mean... *dinner*? Or...
    JEN. No, Ty! Not dinner! Or okay, maybe dinner, too.
    TY. I'm sorry.

(JEN grabs her own hair. Starts walking to the door, walks back to TY.)

JEN. You know what...?

(Again she starts walking to the door, back to TY. To the door, back to TY.)

TY. Are you okay?

JEN. Shut up! Look at me! I don't know which way to go. Ever. This is your fault, Ty. Everything is your fault.

TY. I know.

JEN. I'm so stupid!

TY. You're not stupid. I'm stupid.

JEN. *(Trying to calm down)* Okay. Okay. Look. Let's just... Let's just... You know. Franny told me... She told me you were going to...

TY. Oh, God, Jen, I'm sorry...

JEN. Well what? What do you want? Ty, just look at me and tell me... I hate you right now so fucking much but if you can look at me and tell me... Tell me that you're at least the person I think I know and not some... some.... I DON'T KNOW... Can you look at me...? Can you tell me anything? *(Beat)* Ty.

(JEN exits.)

TY. *(To audience)* What happened to me? Where did I go wrong?

Scene 18
Halfsies

(BECCA and TY in a park. They sit on a bench drinking coffee.)

TY. I want to pay for the whole thing.
BECCA. No. Half is better.
TY. I'd *really like* to pay for the whole thing.
BECCA. No.
TY. Why not?
BECCA. Because I said so.
TY. Don't be a brat.
BECCA. What are you, gonna get *stern* with me?
TY. You don't have the money, I have the money. I'm going to give you the money.
BECCA. I have plenty of money.
TY. How?
BECCA. I'm rich.
TY. Becca.
BECCA. So forget it.

(Beat)

TY. I want to go with you.
BECCA. No way.
TY. Why not?
BECCA. You *want* a lot of things.
TY. Yes. I do.
BECCA. Look, I appreciate everything. But just give me

space on this. Give me half the money and then, you know, walk away. Wash your hands of me.

TY. I don't want to wash my hands of you.

BECCA. Why not?

TY. Because we're connected. We didn't want this to happen, but just because it did doesn't mean I suddenly don't want anything to do with you.

BECCA. Do you want to marry me?

(Beat)

TY. No.

BECCA. Do you want to *date* me?

TY. It's not like that—

BECCA. Because I don't want to date you.

TY. Okay.

BECCA. All I *really* want is for you to write me a check for half the amount and then I just don't want to hang out anymore. I mean, the semester is done. I'm no longer your student. So I don't have to see you anymore.

TY. You should just let me come with you.

BECCA. Whatev.

TY. Whatev?

BECCA. Whatev.

TY. *(Angry)* Why do you always shorten every fucking word?

BECCA. I don't.

TY. You do!

BECCA. Whatev.

TY. Is it some generational thing? What, are you kids too

lazy you can't even finish a word? Finishing words... It's like Too Many Consonants. It's so *ridic.*

BECCA. Oh, poor old Ty can't relate to youth culture. A month ago you understood me. Now you're my dad.

TY. That's not—

BECCA. You can't get three girls pregnant at the same time and then expect them to *like* you.

(Beat. They drink their coffee.)

TY. I'm not a bad person.

BECCA. Whatev. *(Beat)* What are they doing anyhow? Maureen and... what's her face?

TY. Jen.

BECCA. Jen.

TY. Maureen's going to have the baby. Her husband left her.

BECCA. That sucks.

TY. Jen, I don't know. She won't talk to me. *(Beat)* I loved her.

BECCA. Guess you'll have plenty to write about.

(Beat)

TY. Becca, can I tell you something?

BECCA. Uh oh.

TY. I don't know. I just... I need to... You should know how easy it is to ruin yourself, how the smallest things can change who you are. How choices can damage you.

(BECCA gets up.)

BECCA. I don't need any more lessons from you Ty. But I appreciate the thought. Take care of yourself. *(She starts to leave.)* And send me a check.

(BECCA exits. TY watches her go.)

Scene 19
Absolution

(Ty's apartment. TY enters. MAUREEN is sitting, waiting for him. TY turns on the light, surprised to see her. She's visibly pregnant.)

TY. Jesus! You scared me.

MAUREEN. Hello. Sorry. Didn't mean to.

TY. You sit with the lights off?

MAUREEN. I'm tired. The lights are bright.

TY. God. You want a drink? Or, you know, some ice cream?

MAUREEN. I need you to sign these papers. I gave them to you three months ago.

TY. Okay! Jeez. You scared the shit out of me.

MAUREEN. Where've you been?

TY. I've been out walking around in circles. Okay? Is that okay? And then I get a heart attack because you're sitting here waiting for me in the dark like Dracula or something. How'd you get in here anyhow?

MAUREEN. I just hopped on over. Your back door was unlocked. Sign the papers.

TY. What's the rush?

MAUREEN. I'm leaving in a few days. I'm moving. I told you this.

TY. To Boston.

MAUREEN. Yes.

TY. Who moves to *Boston*?

MAUREEN. Sign there. Your name. You know what it says. *Absolve* yourself.

TY. When I was a little kid, I was always terrified when I'd go up to my bedroom at night. I always thought Dracula'd be waiting for me. Just sitting there at my desk, waiting. I think I'm still afraid of that.

MAUREEN. Well here I am.

TY. My new vampire. Vampriss. Whatev.

MAUREEN. I want you to sign the papers.

TY. It's just so final!

MAUREEN. You should have seen your face when I first asked you... You were so relieved.

TY. I feel different now!

MAUREEN. I really don't care.

TY. Why not?

MAUREEN. Because I don't. Sign the papers and I'll leave you alone.

TY. Why is everyone being so mean to me?!

MAUREEN. We had an agreement.

TY. I don't want to sign.

MAUREEN. It doesn't matter what you want anymore. You had what you wanted. Plenty of it.

TY. Maureen...
MAUREEN. What.
TY. I want to...

(TY touches her and brings her close to him as if to kiss her.)

MAUREEN. Stop. What are you doing.
TY. I want to hold you for a second.
MAUREEN. Ty please just— *(TY kisses her. MAUREEN doesn't kiss back, nor does she pull away. After the kiss they look at each other. MAUREEN shoves him away.)* Don't do that.
TY. I'm sorry.
MAUREEN. I don't need this from you, Ty.
TY. What's your *problem*? I'm just—
MAUREEN. SIGN! The papers!

(TY looks at MAUREEN and then quickly rips the papers up into shreds.)

MAUREEN. *WHAT ARE YOU DOING?!*
TY. I don't want to sign them.
MAUREEN. Are you out of your mind!
TY. I come in here, you've broken in. I try to be nice to you, try to be affectionate, you know, and you just act like some mean old... I mean you're mean.
MAUREEN. I'm allowed to be mean! You are too much.
TY. What's the big deal?
MAUREEN. The big *deal?*
TY. Yeah! The big deal! What's the fucking big deal!
MAUREEN. The big deal is I am falling apart, Ty! Nick *left*

me. He took Augie and if I want to see... If I want to even *see* my
son with any regularity, I have to move up there. To Boston
where Nick and his whole family—who hate me now—live.
And... I know you can't understand this. But it hurts, okay?

TY. I know it hurts.

MAUREEN. Oh, you don't know shit.

TY. Yeah? Well I know it's a good thing your husband left
you. You didn't love him, he didn't love you—

MAUREEN. He took my son.

TY. Yeah, well he was adopted. *(MAUREEN slaps TY hard
across the face.)* I'm sorry. Maureen... I didn't mean that.

MAUREEN. He's my *son.*

TY. I know. I'm sorry I said that and I'm sorry I ripped up
those papers. I'll sign them. I mean, you gave me a copy, I'll sign
that.

MAUREEN. Send it to my lawyer.

(MAUREEN turns to go.)

TY. Wait! Maureen, wait...

(TY goes down on knees.)

MAUREEN. What are you doing?

TY. I messed up. I messed up my life.

MAUREEN. Yeah, no kidding.

TY. I need your help.

MAUREEN. You're crazy.

(She turns to leave.)

TY. I'm serious! Wait! I have something deep hanging over me. And I think it corrupted me and made me into a terrible person, the person you know now. The person you hate. And okay, I'm fine with that. I'm bad. But I need to, I don't know, reconcile. What do I do?

MAUREEN. *I* don't know. Why are you asking me this?

TY. Just tell me something! I'm trying to fix my life. I want to be good. What do I do? Can't you tell me anything? *(MAUREEN exits.)* Maureen! I'm sorry!

Scene 20
What Happened Between Us

(Franny and Seth's apartment. FRANNY is exercising along to an exercise video. TY enters.)

FRANNY. What do you want?

TY. Can I come in?

FRANNY. Seth isn't here.

TY. I'm not here to see Seth,

FRANNY. Jen's not here.

TY. I'm not here to see Jen.

FRANNY. Well, that leaves me.

TY. Can I come in?

FRANNY. I feel so needed. What do you want.

TY. I need to talk to you.

(Beat)

FRANNY. ...*Well?*

TY. How's Jen?

FRANNY. Jen who?

TY. Can you be normal for once?

FRANNY. Please don't make yourself at home, Ty. You should not feel this is a safe place for you. It's not.

TY. Gee, thanks, Fran. You're so sweet. *(Beat)* This is hard.

FRANNY. What?

TY. I have to come clean. About everything. To Seth and Jen. About us.

(Beat)

FRANNY. You must be out of your fucking mind.

TY. I'm not. But I wanted to tell you first.

FRANNY. You're going to *tell* Seth and Jen. *Now?* A year later?

TY. This is what I want to talk about.

FRANNY. Talk then!

TY. What we did... Franny, what happened between us...

FRANNY. We made a deal, Ty.

TY. I know we did.

FRANNY. It was a stupid drunken thing. *In the kitchen.* It didn't happen. We decided it *never happened.* We made a deal and we put it behind us. End of story, Ty. End of story.

TY. It's not behind us. It's right here. Right now.

FRANNY. What do you want? What are you trying to hold over me?

TY. Nothing. I just need to do this. I need to come clean.

FRANNY. Take a shower, then!

TY. It was a sin. And I've been feeling it for the past year, but I haven't faced it. Real sin stays with us. And I have to deal with it.

FRANNY. Holy shit. Are you born-again? Because if you are? If you're a born-again little freak, you can get the fuck out of my apartment right now.

TY. I love her, Franny. I've always loved her and I don't know why I did what I did with you. I don't. But I loved her then and I love her now and I'm trying to come clean and I want her back.

FRANNY. That's sweet, Ty. That's so sweet my teeth hurt.

TY. I used to be a normal person, you know? But that night fucked me up. You corrupted something in me.

FRANNY. I *what*?

TY. I don't know what it was, but I turned a corner and I can never get back.

FRANNY. I *corrupted* something in you? What did I do, pop your cherry?

TY. No.

FRANNY. We just made a huge mistake is all. Me and Seth are about to get *married*. God knows it'll never happen again and so just drop it! It *never* happened.

TY. It happened, Franny. Look, I'm not here to argue with you or to ask your permission. I'm telling Seth and I'm telling Jen.

FRANNY. So why are you telling me? Why did you come over and run this by me first?

TY. I thought you should know.

FRANNY. Bullshit. That's way too courteous for you, Ty. You know what I think? I think you're here because you want me to talk you out of it.

TY. That's ridiculous.

FRANNY. What can I say that will convince you to shut the fuck up?

TY. Nothing! I'm going to tell them.

FRANNY. Why? What do you want? What do you expect to get out of this? What is telling them going to get you?

TY. I want to feel like I haven't irrevocably messed up my life. *(Beat)* I want the four of us to be like we used to be like. I mean, remember how we were? For a brief moment, we were like a family. And then you and I had to screw everything up.

FRANNY. You think we screwed things up then? Wait till you blabber to Seth and Jen NOW. That's it. Say goodbye to everything.

TY. I have to make things right.

FRANNY. Allright, Allright, Allright. Fuck, Fuck, Fuck.

(FRANNY stares at TY, walks to a table, takes out a white envelope, brings it to him and holds it out.)

TY. What's this.

FRANNY. An invitation to our wedding.

TY. What, I'm invited now?

FRANNY. Yeah. And you're best man, too. So start thinking about your toast.

TY. What are you talking about?

FRANNY. You want things to go back to the way they were? Then start using your stupid idiot head, Ty. You're coming to the wedding, you're gonna be Seth's best man, you're gonna walk down the aisle with pregnant Jen, you're gonna be sweet and nice and charming and all that shit you always pull and you're going to keep your fucking mouth shut about things that don't need to be said.

TY. I don't see how that will fix things.

FRANNY. You can either put the pieces back together or you can blow everything apart.

TY. You would do this for me?

FRANNY. Do we have a deal?

TY. What about Paco?

FRANNY. Fuck Paco. He can be the ring bearer. He won't know the difference. *(TY looks at the invitation, thinking.)* This is a deal I'm making with you, Ty. If you're serious about all this shit, you'll think about the future and not about your stupid guilt.

TY. You think Jen will... You think she'll take me back?

FRANNY. I don't know, Ty, I'm not a fucking mind reader. Do we have a deal?

TY. Yeah. *(TY takes the invitation and turns to leave.)* Franny... Thank you.

FRANNY. You're welcome. Now go away. I have to do my pilates.

Scene 21
Toast

(TY stands center stage in his suit holding a microphone and a glass of champagne.)

TY. We were fourteen years old, Seth and I, and we were at the mall. Hanging out, drinking cokes. Like fourteen-year-olds do at the mall. It was summer and we were bored and sitting by one of those mall fountains, stealing pennies from under the water.

This woman walked up to the fountain. She was beautiful. And she looked at the fountain, went into a coin purse, found a nickel, made a wish, and flipped it into the fountain.

Seth and I watched this. We couldn't take our eyes off of her.

Anyhow, then she walked away. We had cleaned out the fountain, and so the only coin left in the water was that woman's nickel. I tried to reach in and get it, but it was too far. I couldn't reach it. But Seth was still watching the woman walk away. And then, as if he were dreaming, Seth said to me:

"You know, I just love women."

And I said, yeah, she was hot.

And then Seth said:

"Isn't it amazing to think that someday, we could hang out with a woman like that? Someday, a woman like that might want to date us? Or marry us?"

And I said, yeah, that would be awesome.

And Seth just shook his head and said, more to himself, "Man. I just love women."

Here's the reason I'm telling this story today. Seth was

wrong. Seth didn't love "women". Seth didn't love that woman at
the fountain. Seth loved the *idea* of a woman that might be perfect in his every estimation. That day, stealing pennies from a
fountain, Seth suddenly understood that life was only worth liv-
ing if there remained the possibility of finding that perfect match,
that missing piece, that most beautiful and perfect of mates with
whom to share his life.

He has.

I want to raise my glass to them and to their families...

and also to the maid of honor...

And I want to say...

I want to say...

Salud.

Scene 22
Pull of the Moon

*(JEN stands outside the wedding reception looking at the moon.
She is very pregnant. TY enters.)*

TY. Look at that moon.

JEN. That's what I was doing.

TY. Strong enough to pull the tides, to move the oceans. No
wonder it can mess with our heads. *(Reminiscing)* You remember
that moon, that one time when we were at the—

JEN. Yes. I do. Of course I do. *(Beat)* You made a very nice toast.

TY. I winged it.

JEN. I figured.

TY. Yeah.

JEN. Yeah.

TY. So what's going on?

JEN. Oh, nothing. I'll be a mother in about a month. I'm gonna have a little girl.

TY. *It's a girl?*

JEN. Yes.

TY. Jen...

JEN. Don't you get sappy, Ty. I really don't want to hear it. I don't want to hear *you.*

(Beat)

TY. I want to marry you. Jen... I want to get married.

JEN. You make me sick.

TY. Is that a no?

JEN. Why would you tell me that?

TY. What, propose to you?

JEN. No, you didn't propose. Proposals inquire. You simply stated. *I want to marry you. I want to get married.* A litany of wants. No proposal. No question.

TY. Well, then, do you *want*—

JEN. No, I don't want to marry you. Jesus. I want to *not see* you.

TY. Well, I figured that. You haven't returned my calls... or my e-mails... or my text messages...

JEN. You had a chance to explain yourself. You had a

chance to make things better and you didn't. So, thanks for the *text messages* but I've moved on.

(Beat)

> TY. I'm sorry.
> JEN. I know.

(TY touches Jen's stomach tenderly. She allows him.)

> TY. It's a girl.
> JEN. Yes.

(The baby kicks. JEN reacts and TY feels it as well. He's astounded by this.)

> TY. What are we going to name her?
> JEN. We?
> TY. Well, I mean... Jeez. She's my daughter too.
> JEN. Are you kidding me?
> TY. I mean, I'm not trying to be antagonistic here, Jen! But you're got to realize that I'm connected to you, okay? Maybe you hate me and never want to see me, but she's my daughter too. She's OUR daughter. And I don't want it to come down to this, but I mean, legally I could get partial custody if I wanted to.
> JEN. *Legally.* Jesus. I can't believe you're going to talk LAW with me. You won't get partial custody or anything like it.
> TY. Why not?
> JEN. Courts favor the child's best interest.
> TY. I'm her father.

JEN. You're nothing. We go to court? I'll demonstrate that you're incapable of performing parental duties. You're unwilling to actively participate in the raising of a child. And conditions exist that would substantially interfere with the exercise of joint legal custody: For example, that I would kill you.

TY. What's that supposed to mean?

JEN. It means I'm a lawyer. Remember? I passed the bar. Somehow, in your absence, I got my life together.

(She exits. SETH enters.)

SETH. Best friend... Best man...

TY. Yeah, dude, what's wrong with you? Are you wasted? *(SETH stares at TY.)* What?

SETH. "What?" "What?"

TY. What's wrong?

SETH. You tell me.

TY. Where do I start? Jen... She...

SETH. Franny told me.

TY. Told you what?

SETH. Guess.

(Beat)

TY. She fucking told you? *I* was gonna tell you!

SETH. But you didn't. You didn't.

TY. Seth...

SETH. To get this on my wedding day! Two hours before the ceremony.

TY. She told you before the ceremony?

SETH. Yes.

TY. Aren't the bride and groom not supposed to see each other before the ceremony?

SETH. Yeah.

TY. Isn't that like bad luck?

SETH. She needed to tell me before we got married.

TY. That's pretty low, man. *(Beat)* Well, look: I apologize.

SETH. Oh great. That's great, Ty.

TY. I'm sorry.

SETH. You fucked my wife!

TY. She wasn't your wife then.

SETH. We were engaged!

TY. Listen—

SETH. No. No. I'm done with you. *We're* done. I want you out of here. Out of my life.

TY. We're best friends!

SETH. Well, you can find yourself a new best friend.

TY. I can... Seth, what are you, in the third grade?

SETH. Oh, and okay, let's just pretend, for old times sake, that I forgive you for that. Because you're *such a good friend.* Here you are all forgiven and you're my Best Man and you're up there and you give this fucking toast. This nice fucking toast.

TY. What, now you have a problem with my toast?

SETH. How self-absorbed can you *get* man?

TY. What are you talking about?

SETH. Your cute little toast? You made me you and you me. You switched the roles! You told a story about yourself. You were the one poeticizing about that woman. Those were your lines! I was the one trying to get that fucking nickel.

TY. That's not true. That's—

SETH. You couldn't even think of something interesting or nice to say about *me*. So you just gave me *your* lines. I don't want your lines, man. I'm through with you. Take it easy, asshole. Have a nice life.

(SETH exits.)

TY. That's a cliché exit line, dude! I can't let you go out like that! Come back and say something cold-blooded! Tell me off, dude! Bitch me out! Say something smart! I'll give you a second chance! Come back and hit me! Punch me in the face! Seth! I deserve it! Come on! You can't just leave. Seth, come back.

(TY walks to bench and sits and puts his face in his hands.)

Scene 23
All This and More

(Ty's office. He takes a map of Pangea and hangs it up. Stares at it. Turns and speaks to the audience.)

TY. You know that time in your life? When your future is rich and ripe and full of possibility? And you haven't done anything to taint it yet? And you have virgin soil beneath your feet and the world is a good place and you are a good person?

And then you eat the forbidden fruit. And you're banished

from that perfect place because you're not worthy of it any more. And so what do you do then?

You live in shame. You cover your nakedness, avert your eyes, cultivate secrets, you tear the world to pieces, start nations, start civilizations. Fuck. Have children. Spread your seed. Create a new world, where new people will have the opportunity to stand in a new garden of Eden and proceed to fail all over again. Just like you did. Just like you did

(BECCA enters.)

    BECCA. Hi.
    TY. Oh. Hi.
    BECCA. Hi.
    TY. Come in.
    BECCA. I was just passing by. I have to be somewhere.
    TY. Oh. Hi.
    BECCA. *(Re: map of Pangaea)* What is that? Is that Russia?
    TY. No. No, it's Pangaea.
    BECCA. It looks like Russia.
    TY. No, it's not Russia, it's Pangaea. It's the way the world used to look when all the continents were connected. It's speculative, it's not real, it's... Anyhow. How've you been?
    BECCA. I just wanted to stop by and say congrats on the book.
    TY. Oh, thanks!
    BECCA. I got it.
    TY. You bought one?
    BECCA. Yeah.
    TY. Great! *(Beat)* Do you like it?

BECCA. I liked *Labyrinth* better.

TY. Look, I hope they're not...

BECCA. Hey, write what you know. You know?

TY. There's a lot of you in there.

BECCA. Oh, you think? *(Beat)* Anyway, I saw you dedicated the book to...

TY. Yeah... *(Beat)* Yeah.

BECCA. Have you seen them?

TY. No.

BECCA. Oh. Well, I wrote a new poem.

TY. You did?

BECCA. Yeah. Wanna hear it?

TY. Sure.

BECCA. I have it memorized. Here it goes:

"This is just to say...
I have eaten
the plums
that were in
the icebox

and which
you were probably
saving
for breakfast

Forgive me
they were delicious
so sweet
and so cold"

    (Beat) Do you like it? It's my best poem, I think.

TY. Becca, you didn't write that.

BECCA. Yes I did.

TY. No, that's William Carlos Williams.

BECCA. No, I wrote it.

TY. No, you didn't.

BECCA. I wrote it. It's my best poem.

TY. No you *didn't*. Becca...

BECCA. Yes I did. Don't tell me I didn't write it. I wrote it.

TY. No you DIDN'T!

(Beat)

BECCA. I know, I'm just shitting you.

TY. Oh.

BECCA. You're such a spaz.

TY. Yeah, I know.

BECCA. I know it was William Carlos Williams! I'm not stupid, you know.

TY. I know.

BECCA. We studied it in your class.

TY. I know. *(TY stands up.)* Can I tell you something?

BECCA. What?

TY. I realized... I don't know... But I realized... *(Re: Pangaea)* This map... it was Jen's dissertation. I got it off the internet. Isn't that crazy?

BECCA. Yeah. Crazy.

TY. I mean. I don't know. It's pretty amazing when you think about it. How the world used to look. *(Beat)* God, I don't... I don't even know what I'm trying to say.

BECCA. Think about it. It'll come to you. I gotta run.

TY. Hey. Do you want to... You know, get a drink?
BECCA. I'm not old enough to drink.
TY. Coffee.
BECCA. Probably not.

(BECCA leaves. Beat. TY picks up a book.)

TY. This is my new book. My new book of poems. It's dedicated to my daughters. It's titled "The Imperative Promiscuity of
the New Father of Humankind." It's a little wordy. And I worried
that it would do poorly. Instead, it's a best seller.

There's no feeling in the world like writing a book. To work
on something, to put your labor and love into it and then to get it
published... When you hold your book in your hands... there's
nothing like it. It's like holding your... *(Beat)*

Nobody reads poetry, but people like this book. I think they
like it because the poems link together and tell one narrative tale.
It's about after the apocalypse. There are only fifteen people left
in the entire world. Fourteen of them are women between the
ages of fourteen and forty. And there is one man. Naturally, the
man must copulate extensively with each woman. It is up to them
to work together and re-create humanity.

I like it because it's his job. It's his duty. He's doing the right
thing.

It doesn't matter if he's unkind! It doesn't matter what anyone thinks about him, because everyone is dead, wiped out, exter-
minated by the indifferent apocalypse. The future of mankind is
dependant on his seed, his come, his dick. And he fucks for mankind, for humanity and he's doing the right thing.

It's his job.

I'm telling you! Please believe me.
Please believe me.
He's doing the right thing.

*(TY looks at the book and then throws the book as hard as he can
against the wall.)*

The End

PROPS AND FURNITURE LIST

PROPS:
Notebook—Becca
Bonnybell chapstick—Becca
Sugarfree gum—Becca
Toys to fit in coffee table—Ty
Medium sized, rubber shiny ball—Ty
3 or 4 red markers—Ty
3 or 4 perforated legal pads with pages ripped each night—Ty
Large stack of wedding invitations, one addressed to Ty
    Greene—Franny
Box of saltines, eaten each night—Jen
Large and possibly old photograph of Franny's parent's wed-
    ding—Franny
Stack of student's papers—Ty
Pens, pencils, student papers, books, etc.—Ty
Bag—Becca
Crumpled poem—Becca
Binder for poetry—Ty
6 Plastic cups of wine—Ty, Jen, Fran, Seth
Red bottle of wine—Becca
Cell phone—Becca
Apron—Ty
Pickels served in a bowl—Ty
Bowl for pickles—Ty
New, unopened box of condoms—Franny
6 Pack of beer of Amstel Light—Franny
Bag—Franny
Lighter—Franny
Plastic bag for condoms and beer—Franny

Turkey jerkey—Seth
Pack of Parliament Light cigarettes—Seth
Backpack—Jen
Bike helmet—Jen
Pictionary—Seth
Cup of coffee—Ty
Bottle of water—Becca
Legal papers ripped each night—Maureen
Pen—Maureen
Ashtray—Franny
Microphone on stand—Ty
Glass of Champagne—Ty
Glass of Champagne—Seth
Map—Ty
Book—Ty

FURNTITURE:
Sofa/love seat, small
Coffee table, opens to hold toys
Desk
Round table
Additional small table for photograph and other props
2 chairs
2 additional chairs

THE SCENE
Theresa Rebeck

Little Theatre / Drama / 2m, 2f / Interior Unit Set
A young social climber leads an actor into an extra-marital affair, from which he then creates a full-on downward spiral into alcoholism and bummery. His wife runs off with his best friend, his girlfriend leaves, and he's left with... nothing.

"Ms. Rebeck's dark-hued morality tale contains enough fresh insights into the cultural landscape to freshen what is essentially a classic boy-meets-bad-girl story."
- *New York Times*

"Rebeck's wickedly scathing observations about the sort of self-obsessed New Yorkers who pursue their own interests at the cost of their morality and loyalty."
- *New York Post*

"The Scene is utterly delightful in its comedic performances, and its slowly unraveling plot is thought-provoking and gut-wrenching."
- *Show Business Weekly*